The Shrunken Goblin

Written by Nelson R. Elliott

Illustrated by Sam McKinnon

KDP ISBN: 9781792612305

v2.0

DEDICATION

To my children. Be discerning.

Once upon a time, there lived a poor fisherman. He was a widower with three children and lived a long way from town in small house at the bottom of a lighthouse. When he was at sea, his children would keep the lighthouse lit to guide his boat back in and keep him from running aground on the rocky shore.

His children were named Adam, Noah, and Chloe. Adam was the eldest, followed by Noah, and Chloe was the youngest.

The fisherman always tried to be home before the winter gales blew in, but, one autumn, the winter gales arrived early and he was caught at sea. The children were very worried about their father.

Fall turned into winter and the gales did not stop. The wind blew and the snow piled up. The children slowly ran out of food and money. They soon turned their attention from their father and began worrying about what they would eat.

One day, Adam sent Chloe into town with the last silver dollar to buy a loaf of brown bread and a bag of cornmeal. On her way back, she saw something small and green struggling through the deep snow on the road. She stopped to help the poor creature and saw it was goblin, no bigger than a mouse.

Chloe's father had told her tales of goblins and she knew they could be treacherous, dangerous creatures. This one was very small, though. What harm could it do? Besides, Chloe was moved to pity by the sad sight of the little thing clawing its way through the snow. It would surely die if Chloe abandoned it and so, against her father's warnings, she picked it up and brought it back to the lighthouse.

When she returned, she warmed the poor goblin up, giving it a washrag to use as a blanket and feeding it crumbs of brown bread. It was very grateful.

As the three children looked on, the goblin stood on the table.

"You have saved me from certain death," it proclaimed, at the top of its tiny lungs, "I will reward you as best I can. I will grant each of you a wish. I am small, though, so my powers are limited. What do you want?"

Adam wished for a new pocketknife to whittle with. Noah wished for peppermint candy to eat after dinner. Chloe wished for a silver dollar, with which to buy more bread.

The goblin closed its eyes, jumped three times, and clapped its hands. There was a small pop and a puff of smoke and the children's wishes appeared in front of them on the table.

The children were very impressed. They were quite excited by their new gifts and amazed at the goblin's talent. But the goblin seemed very sad still.

"What's the matter?" asked Chloe, "Aren't you warm and full?"

"Yes," the goblin replied, "but that's exactly the problem. You have saved my life and in return I can only offer trinkets. You deserve so much more." It paused and sat down on the edge of a candlestick holder. "You know, if I were larger, I could grant you better wishes. Will you give me the loaf of bread you have? Tomorrow I will repay it tenfold."

Chloe discussed this with her brothers. It was their last meal, but the goblin had already proved its powers. They had nothing to lose by giving it a chance. What did starving one day faster matter? They gave the bread to the goblin as they went to bed that night.

The next morning they awoke to find the bread and the goblin gone.

"Ah, we fell for a crummy goblin trick," complained Adam. Just as he finished saying that though, the door opened and the goblin came in from the winter storm outside. It was now the size of a dwarf and was carrying a load of firewood.

It put the new logs on the fire and then turned to the children. "Now that I am bigger, I can grant you better wishes. What would you like?"

This time, Adam wished for a new axehead, with which to chop firewood faster. Noah asked for a hot, sticky cinnamon bun to eat for breakfast. Chloe wished for a hog to raise and butcher.

The goblin closed its eyes, jumped three times, and clapped its hands. There was a bang and a cloud of smoke and the gifts appeared.

Just as before, the children were happy, but the goblin was still sad. "It is still less than you deserve. If only I were bigger yet, I could grant you better wishes."

"We can roast the hog for dinner," suggested Noah. They all agreed.

Adam took his new axehead and butchered the hog. They roasted it on a spit all day until dinnertime. All four ate and ate. The children had their fill long before the hog was gone, but the goblin just kept eating. It was still eating when the children went to bed.

The next morning, the children awoke to find the goblin just finishing the hog. It was now enormous. It could still walk around in the house, but was bigger than any man the children had ever seen. It was in a very good mood.

"Children," the goblin boomed, "at last I have the power to repay your kindness fully. I can grant each of you any wish."

At once, all three shouted, "Bring our father home!"

The goblin was crestfallen. "Alas, that is still too large a task. I have spoken too soon. I must be larger still to grant you that wish. What else would you wish for?"

The children were disappointed too, but decided to make the best of the situation. Adam wished for a repeating rifle to hunt with. Noah wished for a feast to eat and be merry with. Chloe wished for a cow, to provide milk and butter through the winter.

The goblin closed it eyes, jumped three times, banging its head on the ceiling each time, and clapped its hands. There was an enormous boom that shook the whole house and a dense smoke filled the air.

The children coughed and clawed their way to the doors and windows to let the smoke out. As the air cleared, they could see the goblin had granted their wishes as before.

Adam's rifle hung over the fireplace. Chloe's cow mooed from a pen behind the lighthouse. And Noah's feast filled the little house. There was chowder, lobster, clams, bread, potatoes, corn, apples, squash, cranberries, pie, johnnycakes, and more! All four sat down to eat. They ate and ate and ate through the entire day.

The food seemed to magically replenish itself and the children stopped eating to go to bed long before the food was gone.

They awoke in the morning to find the house strewn with empty plates, dirty forks, and crumbs. They did not see the goblin.

As her brothers cleaned, Chloe went outside, into a growing winter gale, to milk the cow. There the goblin lay, leaning against the house, now far too large to fit inside.

Chloe was surprised how large it had grown, but was also excited. "Now you can bring our father back!" she cried happily.

"Perhaps," grunted the goblin lazily. "I am still a bit peckish. Perhaps we could have another meal?"

Chloe was very annoyed, "You are breaking your promise. Besides, we have nothing left to eat!"

"Not true, we have a cow," retorted the goblin.

"Yes, but we need the cow's milk during the winter."

"Well, would you rather have milk or have your father back?"

Chloe went inside and discussed this dilemma with her brothers. Adam, still wary of goblin tricks, did not want to give up the cow. Chloe was torn between missing her father and wanting the cow's milk for the winter. Noah was hungry for beef, however, and lobbied his sister heavily with visions of steaks, stews, and stroganoffs. So, when they put it to a vote, it was decided to slaughter and cook the cow.

The goblin, being massive now, ate the cow very quickly. When he was done, the children begged him to grant their last wish.

"Surely, now you are big enough to walk through the ocean water. You are so tall, you can surely see the ship's mast a long way off," they said.

The goblin laughed, "Foolish children. I obeyed you when I was small and dependent on your good graces. Now, I am large and powerful and you will be my servants."

It produced a bag of silver coins. The bag looked small in the goblin's hands, but was actually a small fortune. "Go into town and buy me all the cows at the market. Bring them back and cook me a feast."

The children did as they were told. What else were they to do? They went to market and found three cows for sale. They brought them back to the lighthouse and cooked one cow each day for the next three days.

The goblin got larger and larger. When the cows were gone, the goblin looked around. "I am still hungry! Fetch me more cows!"

"We cannot," said Adam, "we have purchased all the cows in town."

The goblin was unmoved. "Well, what else do you have for me to eat?"

"Nothing, we are quite poor," Noah explained.

"Well, then, I'll eat you!" And with that, the goblin picked Noah up and ate him in two bites.

Chloe and Adam were terrified and ran back inside, where Adam loaded his new rifle. As the goblin clawed through the door, he went to the window and aimed, shooting out one of the goblin's eyes.

The goblin roared in pain and seized Adam through the window. "I will eat all of your wretched family," it cried.

"Little girl," it yelled to Chloe, "I will eat your last brother, then I will eat you, then I will wade into the ocean and find your father and eat him too."

Chloe saw that her brother had dropped his rifle when the goblin had grabbed him, so she picked it up and went outside. The goblin laughed at her, "You will have to do better than that to defeat me. Your brother could not kill me with it and you will not be able to either."

But Chloe did not listen. Determined to save her brother, she aimed carefully while the goblin boasted about its size, its thick skin, and its magical powers. Finally, she fired and shot out the goblin's other eye.

Again, the goblin roared in pain. It dropped Adam to the ground and tried to run away. It was now blind, however and stumbled to and fro in the wind and snow. As it did, it knocked over the lighthouse tower, sending it crashing to the ground and extinguishing its light.

At last, the goblin stumbled over the cliffs and fell down into the ocean.

Adam and Chloe ran to the edge of the cliff to see the goblin wading in the surf. Over the storm and waves, they could hear it cursing them. Then, the goblin stopped. It put his hands over its bloody eyes, jumped three times, and then clapped its hands.

There was a terrific bolt of lightning and peal of thunder and just like that, the goblin's eyes were back. It glared up at the two children and then began wading toward the cliff.

Adam and Chloe watched solemnly, sure that the goblin would finish them once it had climbed back up the cliff. But, as they stood saying their goodbyes to each other, a ship appeared through the driving snow. It had become lost when the lighthouse was extinguished and was now being driven toward the cliffs by the wind.

As it neared the rocky shore, the ship's prow plunged into the goblin's back. The goblin screamed and caught on fire. As it burned and smoke filled the air, the goblin shrank - smaller and smaller and smaller until it simply fell into the water.

As the goblin disappeared, the remains of the ship ran aground, its sails in tatters. There was nothing the children could do for it in the storm, so they returned to the house and went to bed without dinner.

The next morning, the storm had passed and the children realized it was their father's ship stuck on the rocks. They made a rope ladder and sent it down the cliffside for him and he climbed up.

He was saddened to hear of Noah's fate and to see the state of his lighthouse, but through the winter he rebuilt the lighthouse. When the spring came, he decided not to set sail again. He got a job in town as a mason and lived happily ever after with his family. They were never hungry again and every year they held a dinner in memory of Noah.

The goblin was never seen again, which was probably just as well for him, as Chloe and Adam had become rather good shots and besides had learned not to feed dangerous creatures.

THE END

ABOUT THE AUTHOR

Nelson lives in New York with his wife and growing family. He works in advertising during the day and writes little fairy tales for his children at night.

Made in the USA
Lexington, KY
11 September 2019